Muffin Man
A Musical

by Camille Harris

Baker's Plays
c/o Samuel French, Inc.
45 West 25th Street
New York, NY 10010
bakersplays.com

MUFFIN MAN was produced at The Greene Theater at Emerson College in Boston, Massachusetts for the Emerson College Honors Program as part of the honor's thesis: *Muffin Man the Musical: Finding Value in the Silly,* May, 2008.

MUFFIN MAN was presented by the Present Company as part of the International Fringe Festival 2009. *MUFFIN MAN* premiered at the Lafayette Theater at 45 Bleeker and was extended as part of the Fring-eNYC Encore Series at the Playhouse Theater. Authorized Company Representative, Scott Sinclair; Pianist, Markus Hauck; Stage Managers, Jalaina Ross and Christina Ventura; Asst. Stage Manager, Caitlin Powers; Lighting Designer/Set, Andy Yanni; Producing Consultant, Bailie Slevin; Creative Consultant, Nikki Rothenburg; Production Assistant: Dana Li; Assistant Producer, Andrew Michaelson; the production was produced and directed by Camille Harris with the following cast:

LYLA	Samantha Blain
JUSTIN	Michael Hill
KEVIN	Scott Johnson
SADIE	Shaye Troha
GARY	Benjamin Fisher
LYLA'S MOM/CUSTOMERS	Alyssa H. Chase
LYLA'S DAD/CUSTOMERS	Ben Prayz
BOBBY/CUSTOMER 2/B	Benjamin K. Glaser
KAT/OTHER CUSTOMERS	Sara Dobrinich

RENTAL MATERIALS

An orchestration consisting of **Piano Vocal Score** will be loaned two months prior to the production ONLY on the receipt of the Licensing Fee quoted for all performances, the rental fee and a refundable deposit.

Please contact Baker's Plays for perusal of the music materials as well as a performance license application.

CHARACTERS

LYLA - Barista at the Perky Coffee Bean, in love with the Muffin Man

JUSTIN - Lyla's "Muffin Man," a neighborhood boy

KEVIN - Procrastinating songwriter, Perky Coffee Bean regular

SADIE - Owner of the Perky Coffee Bean

GARY - Perky Coffee Bean regular, Lyla's family friend

CUSTOMERS - Versatile actors able to play multiple roles including:

    LYLA'S MOM - Kooky mom

    LYLA'S DAD - Supportive father who makes "dad jokes"

    BOBBY - Lyla's adolescent brother, full of angst

    BRIDE - Hysterical Perky Coffee Bean customer

SETTING

The Perky Coffee Bean. A local coffee shop in a small town, Anywhere, USA.

TIME

Summer. The Present.

AUTHOR'S NOTES

Muffin Man is meant to be presented as an adorable and lighthearted show. It's fun to watch the main character Lyla struggle to find the courage to finally speak from her heart. We all have a "Muffin Man," (that one exulted person who we have loved for years) and it's exciting to watch someone finally confront hers.

I believe strongly in the value of the silly. In this world filled with so much sadness, the challenge for me is finding the humor in life and bringing to the stage the most positive of human interactions. I love high energy, musically rich musicals with the kind of music that people sing and whistle when they are happy. I think this show is a reminder that happiness is always a possibility. As the character Sadie says in *Muffin Man,* "Seize the day! Diem Carpe!"

-Camille Harris
2011

SONGS

ACKNOWLEDGMENTS

Emerson College Performing Arts Department, Emerson College Honors Program, The Araca Group, SpringboardNYC and The American Theater Wing, The New York International Fringe Festival, Joanne Lamun & the Peanut Butter Players, Angel, Steve and Sabrina Harris, and Alex Fischer.

Scene 1

*(The lights come half up to reveal a small coffee shop. There are a couple of tables and chairs on stage, and a counter stage left behind which the coffee workers stand. Coffee song vamps. Lights up as we see **LYLA** and **SADIE** talking.)*

SONG 1 - "BARISTA SONG"

SADIE.
> A CAFÉ BARISTA CAN NEVER KEEP STILL,
> HER MIND MUST BE STRAIGHT AND SURE.
> SHE WIPES OFF THE COUNTER,
> WHILE MAKING A DRINK
> FOR SLEEPINESS SHE HAS THE CURE,
> SO CLEAN UP!
> MOVE THROUGH THE ROOM AND PUT ON SMILE!
> SO SHAPE UP!
> PROVE TO THE WORLD THAT YOU'LL GO THE EXTRA MILE!
> THOSE WHO'VE NEVER THOUGHT THEY
> COULD DRINK A WHOLE POT MAY
> FIND IT SOLVES A LATTE PROBLEMS…
> NOW NO ONE NEVER NEEDS ANY SLEEP!
> WORKING EIGHT DAYS A WEEK!
> I BREW SOME GREAT COFFEE, THEN BREW IT AGAIN,
> CAN'T RUN OUT OR EVER BE LATE!
> 'CAUSE WHEN PREPARED WITH PRECISION,
> COFFEE HAS BEAN THE GROUNDS FOR MANY HEATED
> DEBATES!

*(**CUSTOMERS** enter in droves.)*

CUSTOMERS.
> GOOD, GOOD, GOOD, GOOD MORNING!
> *(sip)* Ah.

CUSTOMERS. *(cont.)*

> THANK YOU FOR THE COFFEE, THANK YOU FOR THE COFFEE!
>
> THIS NEEDED SIP HELPS ME ESPRESSO MYSELF!
>
> AFTER ONE TASTE I CAN BE WHO I WANT TO BE!

SADIE.

> SO STICK WITH THE PROGRAM AND GIVE IT A TRY,
>
> FOR YOU HAVE THE QUALITIES,
>
> IF YOU WORK A LITTLE HARDER,
>
> THEN ADD SOME HOT WATER,
>
> YOU'LL BE LADY GREY OF THE TEAS!
>
> FOR WHEN THE RUSH IS OVER,
>
> ALTHOUGH YOU'RE NOT THROUGH,
>
> SEIZE THE DAY.
>
> DIEM CARPE,
>
> AS A BARISTA AT A CAFÉ!

> **(LYLA** *and* **SADIE** *start to set up.)*

> You're going to be perfect! I think you're ready. Here comes someone, oh it's a regular. Try it out.

> *(enter* **GARY***)*

LYLA. Welcome to the Perky Coffee Bean…Gary? What are you doing here?

GARY. Lyla? How long have you been here?

LYLA. Just started. Why is your pant leg rolled up like that?

GARY. I'm a Bike Messenger now.

LYLA. I thought you were at law school.

GARY. I'm doing this now. That's great you work here. I'll be seeing a lot of you!

LYLA. We get messengered?

GARY. Nah, I just come here for coffee. And the muffins are delicious!!

LYLA. Oh really?

GARY. Yes. They're great. Have you tried them?

LYLA. Nah. Not really.

GARY. Oh well, they're from our local bakery.

LYLA. I hadn't noticed.

GARY. You know Justin Baker delivers them right?

LYLA. Who?

GARY. Justin Baker.

LYLA. Oh right. Him. Sure.

SADIE. You know Justin?

GARY. Does she know Justin! They got married when they were babies. All of our families had that cute little ceremony for them. I DJ'd. She's only been in love with him since she was four years old.

LYLA. No I haven't. Anyway, he's a year older, so we've kind of drifted apart. He probably doesn't even know my name anymore.

(enter **JUSTIN***)*

JUSTIN. Lyla! I didn't know you worked here! That's great!

LYLA. Justin…I be my me, ka, can, uh bee…

GARY. Justin! Hey buddy! Look! Lyla works here! She just started today!

JUSTIN. Hey Gary. Here are the muffins for today. We've got cranberry-walnut topped with a little sprinkling of granulated sugar. Mmm, mmm. Then we have a lemon-poppy muffin topped with shaved almond, and, our staple, The Blueberry Muffin. That's my own special recipe. Extra blueberries.

LYLA. I love blueberries.

JUSTIN. That's awesome you work here. I'll be seeing a lot of you.

LYLA. Wonderful.

JUSTIN. Yeah. Cool apron.

LYLA. Thanks. It was my mom's.

JUSTIN. Cool. *(leans on counter)*

> *(beat)*

> **(LYLA** *starts to speak and knocks the cups over.)*

> Hey Sadie.

SADIE. Hey Justie! Getting packed for Dartmouth?

JUSTIN. Can't wait! It's so weird that this is my last summer at the ol' bakery. Dad's sure going to miss me. *(starts to exit)* Oh Sadie, Dad says: "Don't forget the sugar."

(They laugh. **LYLA** *joins in, laughing a little bit too long.* **GARY** *and* **SADIE** *look at her.)*

See you, Lyla!

LYLA. Bye.

*(***JUSTIN*** *exits.)*

GARY. Huh. I guess he does remember you.

SADIE. You guys would be so cute together!

LYLA. No, we wouldn't. He hates my apron anyway.

SADIE. This is so tragic. A little barista in love with the muffin man. *(Suddenly the comedy of the situation dawns on her.)* You're in love with the Muffin Man!

LYLA. Don't say it!

SADIE. Yes, you are! You're in love with the Muffin Man! You're in love with the Muffin Man! *(making up her own version of "The Muffin Man":)*
DO YOU KNOW THE MUFFIN MAN,
THE MUFFIN MAN,
THE MUFFIN MAN,
YOU REALLY LOVE THE MUFFIN MAN
YEAH, YEAH, YEAH, YEAH, YEAH, YEAH.

LYLA. Oh My God! Stop! *(embarrassed, then suddenly serious:)* You're right. I am.

SONG 2 -"MUFFIN MAN"

DO YOU KNOW THE MUFFIN MAN,
THE MUFFIN MAN,
THE MUFFIN MAN,
DO YOU KNOW THE MUFFIN MAN,
WHO LIVES ON DRURY LANE.
OH, WHY DO WE PONDER AND WORRY SO MUCH ABOUT
    THE MUFFIN MAN?
WHY DO WE WORRY ABOUT A SILLY OLD RHYME?
WELL, I KNOW THE MUFFIN MAN
ABOUT A LITTLE TOO WELL,
AND I CAN TELL YOU HE'S MIGHTY FINE.

OH-OH HE MAKES THESE BLUEBERRY MUFFINS THAT MAKE
    ME DROOL
MMM BOY.
AND THEY'RE ALWAYS MADE JUST FOR ME, SO THEY'RE
    NEVER COOL.
BUT I'M JUST A PATRON OF HIS LITTLE SHOP, AND I CAN
    TELL YOU I KNOW I'M A FOOL.
MUFFIN MAN! DO YOU KNOW THE MUFFIN MAN?
'CAUSE MY LIFE'S A DREARY LANE!
OH, WHY DO I PINE SO AND WASTE MY LIFE ON THE MUFFIN
    MAN?
WHY NOT THE CANDLE-STICK MAKER, OR LITTLE BOY BLUE?
BUT HE DOESN'T LOVE ME,
THE WAY THAT I LOVE HIM.
IT SEEMS HE ONLY KNEADS THE DOUGH!
BUT MUFFIN MAN, OH MUFFIN MAN, I LOVE YOU SO.

SADIE. We will totally make him love you by the end of the day. Oh yes! The milk! Be right back.

GARY. Now, if you can just try to get that into one or two sentences, that would be great. Gotta go!

(**SADIE** *and* **GARY** *exit. Enter* **KEVIN.**)

KEVIN. *(calling off stage)* Yeah, yeah man. I'll catch you later. Jeez, these music fans just come out of the woodwork! *(looks up for approval)* Wait. Is Sadie not here? Who are you?

LYLA. I'm Lyla. I'm new.

KEVIN. Ah. Welcome. I'm pretty much what you would call a "regular." I'll be seeing a lot of you. This place is like a zen retreat you know? There is hardly anyone here. Sadie is like my muse and the drink you give me is my elixir. Do you know what I'm saying?

LYLA. I think so…It's nice to meet you. So what's your ushe?

KEVIN. My what? Ushe?

LYLA. Your ushe?

KEVIN. Spell it…

LYLA. Your usual drink. Since you're a regular, I thought you might have a "usual" drink I should learn.

KEVIN. Interesting concept…no, I like to think of myself as a student of the earth. I like to try new things. How about this: you pick.

LYLA. Okay, so…coffee?

KEVIN. Yes. I take it black.

(**LYLA** *hands it to him; he takes a seat.* **SADIE** *enters.*)

SADIE. Hey Lyla.

KEVIN. (*standing up, then sitting back down when she doesn't acknowledge him*) Sadie.

SADIE. Can you keep covering the front? I need to take this call. Great. You'll be great.

(*Enter* **CUSTOMERS A** *and* **B.**)

CUSTOMER A. You know, there's just so much narcissism in this company. I don't know how I'll ever work my way up the ladder.

CUSTOMER B. Oh. Yeah. Definitely. What do you mean?

CUSTOMER A. Well you know, that George guy got promoted, but it's only because his dad is the Vice-President.

CUSTOMER B. So, you're saying he's narcissistic?

CUSTOMER A. No, his dad was.

CUSTOMER B. That doesn't make sense.

CUSTOMER A. Yes, it does. He only got the promotion because of his dad.

CUSTOMER B. Do you mean nepotism? Like when someone favors his or her family?

CUSTOMER A. Yes.

CUSTOMER B. Don't you work in editing?

(*They stare at each other for an extended moment.*)

LYLA. Welcome to the Perky Coffee Bean. Can I help you?

CUSTOMER A. (*still glancing strangely back at* **B**) May I have a house blend with whole milk?

CUSTOMER B. I'll have the same. But with skim.

LYLA. Excellent. Is this together?

CUSTOMER A. Yes. *(begins pulling out his credit card)*

CUSTOMER B. No take mine. *(hands* **LYLA** *his/hers)*

CUSTOMER A. Susan, I'm getting it. Put your card away.

CUSTOMER B. Miss. Take my card. Put your card away. Miss! Take this card.

CUSTOMER A. You'll get a bigger tip if you take mine.

CUSTOMER B. Didn't you just take out a second mortgage?

LYLA. *(laughing warily)* How about you decide. I don't mean to get in the middle of any…..

(**CUSTOMER B** *forces his/her card into her hand,* **CUSTOMER A** *does the same.)*

Wow. I…..

CUSTOMER A. Susan, don't make her uncomfortable.

CUSTOMER B. You're the one making her feel uncomfortable. Slamming your card into her hand like that.

LYLA. I'm fine. Whichever one you want…

CUSTOMER A/B. Mine then.

(**LYLA** *stares at the cards on the counter. Silence.)*

LYLA. How about we do eenie meanie minie mo?

CUSTOMER A. What are we school children?

CUSTOMER B. She is a school child.

LYLA. I'm not a child, I'm a junior. I'm almost in college…

CUSTOMER B. We'll pick a hand.

LYLA. *(putting hands behind her back)* Pick a hand.

CUSTOMER A/B. Left/Left

LYLA. You go first.

CUSTOMER A. Left.

CUSTOMER B. I knew you were going to say that.

LYLA. *(reveals the card in her hand)* Looks like it's yours.

CUSTOMER A. Yes!

CUSTOMER B. Fine, you take it. But I'm getting the next one.

LYLA. *(handing them their drinks)* Here are your drinks. Thanks for dropping in!

CUSTOMER A. Thank you.

CUSTOMER B. It was great seeing you. Have a great day!

CUSTOMER A. You too! Bye!

CUSTOMER B. Bye!

> (**CUSTOMERS** *exit together.*)

CUSTOMER A. *(offstage)* Oh, you're leaving too?

CUSTOMER B. *(offstage)* Yep, well bye.

CUSTOMER A. *(offstage)* Bye.

CUSTOMER B. *(offstage)* Bye.

> (*Enter* **SADIE**)

SADIE. Lyla. You look fabulous. How do you feel?

LYLA. Fine, a little tired maybe.

SADIE. I mean, how do you feel? How does it feel being a barista?

LYLA. It's great to have a job you know.

SADIE. No. Lyla. I mean, how does it feel inside?

LYLA. Fine.

SADIE. You don't feel a warm sensation above your belly button?

LYLA. Not exactly.

SADIE. That's what I feel when I work. There is a warmness that comes with speaking to the masses and helping them. I pride myself on being one of the most efficient and effective people in the service industry. People talk to me, and I know what they want.

KEVIN. Yes, you do.

SADIE. Check out my café skills. This woman may be having a difficult day, but I will help her have an easy and effortless time getting her much deserved caffeine.

> (*enter* **NON-COMMUNICATIVE CUSTOMER**)

Welcome to the Perky Coffee Bean. How are you today?

NON-COMMUNICATIVE CUSTOMER. A Coffee.

SADIE. Great…what size?

NON-COMMUNICATIVE CUSTOMER. Just a coffee.

SADIE. Well, we have small, regular and large.

NON-COMMUNICATIVE CUSTOMER. Large then. *(duh)*

SADIE. Great. And what kind?

NON-COMMUNICATIVE CUSTOMER. Regular.

SADIE. We have House, French Roast, or Decaf.

NON-COMMUNICATIVE CUSTOMER. Decaf? No. House. *(of course)*

SADIE. Great. And do you take milk in your coffee?

NON-COMMUNICATIVE CUSTOMER. Yes.

SADIE. What kind?

NON-COMMUNICATIVE CUSTOMER. *(?)*

SADIE. We have skim, whole, 2%, half and half, soy and rice.

NON-COMMUNICATIVE CUSTOMER. Rice.

SADIE. That's 50 cents extra.

NON-COMMUNICATIVE CUSTOMER. Half and Half then.

SADIE. Great. That will be three dollars.

NON-COMMUNICATIVE CUSTOMER. It says 2.50.

SADIE. What do you mean it says 2.50?

(**NON-COMMUNICATIVE CUSTOMER** *points to board.*)

SADIE. Oh, it says it on the board. Well, that's for regular.

NON-COMMUNICATIVE CUSTOMER. Yes.

SADIE. You ordered a large. Would you like a regular?

NON-COMMUNICATIVE CUSTOMER. Yes.

SADIE. Fine! That will be 2.50 then!

(**NON-COMMUNICATIVE CUSTOMER** *pays and leaves.* **LYLA** *busies herself with the cups)*

That may not have been one of my most eloquent transactions.... I think you can handle it. I'll be in the little office room back there.

(**SADIE** *exits,* **GARY** *enters.)*

GARY. Miss me?

LYLA. Hi Gary!

GARY. May I have your fanciest drink? Crushed ice, the works? I don't have to pay for this, do I? Now that you work here and all and our parents are friends.

LYLA. I may have to ask about that…

GARY. Haha, good one. Thanks. This muffin too. Great.

(**LYLA** *starts making a drink. Blender is loud.*)

So how is your boy?

LYLA. What?

(*The machine is too loud.*)

My what?

GARY. Your boy.

LYLA. My boil?

GARY. No, no. How is your crush?

LYLA. My crotch?

GARY. No your boy!

LYLA. There is not a boil on my…

(*turns off the machine*)

GARY. Your crush.

LYLA. Oh, my crush.

GARY. Yeah.

LYLA. That's weird. Boil sounds nothing like crush.

GARY. Oh, well I had said "Boy" before.

LYLA. Oh, boy!

GARY. Boy!

LYLA. Okay… (*laughing uncomfortably*) My boy. How's that going?

GARY. Yeah.

LYLA. No progress, he hasn't even come back yet.

GARY. Oh well, bummer.

LYLA. I know, it's just never going to happen.

(*She hands him the drink.*)

Enjoy your coffee and muffin and day.

(*enter* **SADIE**)

GARY. Pardon?

LYLA. Enjoy your coffee day. Your day. Muffin. Enjoy your coffee and your day and your muffin. Enjoy your coffee.

*(**SADIE** and **GARY** look at her.)*

GARY. Lyla, do you think you can cool it?

LYLA. Oh no, did I not put enough ice in?

SADIE. I think he meant cool it, as in he's giving you words of advice.

GARY. Relax. You need to just stop freaking about this kid. Take it from me. You should tell him now. I mean it. You see a goodie. Take him. Before it's too late.

SADIE. I agree. If you can stop acting so uncomfortable, it might help your cause.

LYLA. I'm not uncomfortable, I just don't know what to say, and every time I try to make a joke I just sound like a dope and I…

SONG 3 - "CHILL OUT"

SADIE.

SLOW DOWN,
TAKE A LITTLE MOMENT TO BE AND
CHILL OUT
NO ONE LIKES A CRAZY YOU SEE JUST,
COOL OFF
TRUST ME AND I GUARANTEE HE'LL
SEE THAT YOU'RE THE GIRL HE WANTS.

GARY.

I MEAN, SO WHAT?
MAYBE HE'S NOT INTO YOU,

LYLA. What?

GARY.

WHO KNOWS?
HE COULD BE DATING SOMEONE NEW, SO
FIND OUT
LEARN TO SPEAK COHERENTLY AND
SHOW HIM YOU'RE THE GIRL HE WANTS!

SADIE.

> DON'T BE SUCH A WORRIER BABY,
> YOU MUST PERSERVERE.

GARY.

> IN THE LONG RUN YOU DON'T KNOW IF THIS
> BOY WILL STILL BE HERE.

LYLA. What? You don't think this can last?

SADIE.

> CHEER UP
> LOOK AROUND AND GET SOME PERSPECTIVE

GARY.

> GROW UP
> STOP BLUBBERING AND CHOOSE YOUR DIRECTIVE

BOTH.

> RELAX
> YOU'LL NEVER KNOW UNTIL YOU TRY TO
> SHOW HIM YOU'RE THE GIRL HE WANTS.
> YOU COULD BE THE GIRL HE NEEDS.

GARY.

> OR NOT.

SADIE. That's true. You might not be, and that's okay.

LYLA. Ack! You guys! That is not helpful. I might not be? Ahh!!!

GARY. See ya.

> (**GARY** *exits, then comes rushing back in.*)

GARY. Your Muffin Man is on his way here. Just thought I'd let you know.

LYLA. Why is everyone calling him that?

GARY. Well, he's on his way. I would brush your hair if I was you.

> (**LYLA** *runs fingers through hair.*)

> (**JUSTIN** *enters.*)

Remember what I said. Snag this Mr. Muffin Man.

> (*turns and runs into* **JUSTIN** *on his way out*)

There he is!

JUSTIN. Hey.

LYLA. Hey.

JUSTIN. How are you?

LYLA. Good.

JUSTIN. Sorry I was so rushed earlier this morning.

LYLA. Oh it's fine. I was too.

JUSTIN. You were?

LYLA. Well, not really.

JUSTIN. Oh.

> *(silence)*

> **(JUSTIN** *fidgets and looks up at* **LYLA.** *She looks uncomfortably around. They speak at once.)*

JUSTIN.	**LYLA.**
I….	Do…

BOTH. Oh.

> *(silence)*

JUSTIN. You go.

LYLA. No you.

JUSTIN. Um, well *(looks at* **LYLA** *and loses his train of thought)* Uh, oh yeah, my dad wanted a coffee, and my brother wants a tea.

LYLA. Great. *(Doesn't move. Beat.)* Oh, right. Okay. A tea.

JUSTIN. Oh great.

> *(He stands and waits while she works.)*

LYLA.	**JUSTIN.**
Are you…	What do…

LYLA. Hoh kay…

JUSTIN. Whoops, we spoke at the same time again.

> *(He laughs for a second and then stops while* **LYLA** *fidgets uncomfortably.)*

LYLA. So, are you doing anything Friday night?

JUSTIN. Yeah.

LYLA. Oh…what?

JUSTIN. I'm going out with some friends.

LYLA. Well, I'm free Saturday.

JUSTIN. Oh, cool.

LYLA. Are you?

JUSTIN. Yeah… do you want..

LYLA. Do I want to what? *(with anticipation)*

JUSTIN. Do you want a ride home tonight? We might as well carpool now since we're neighbors. *(curses himself when she's not looking)*

LYLA. Oh sure… *(hiding her disappointment)* Here are your drinks.

JUSTIN. Okay. *(pauses)* Thanks. *(starts to leave, pauses)* Good to see you. *(smiles)*

LYLA. You too. *(smiles back)*

(JUSTIN *exits.*)

(SADIE *and* KEVIN *have been observing)*

SADIE. Oh man. He is so into you.

LYLA. What? No he's not.

SADIE. Yes, he is.

KEVIN. He certainly is.

LYLA. You think so?

SADIE. You should ask him out.

KEVIN. Or at least hook up with him.

SADIE. He would be into it.

LYLA. No, he wouldn't, that's the problem!

SADIE. He'd go for it.

KEVIN. He would.

LYLA. He never will.

(enter Lyla's **PARENTS** (**LYLA'S MOM** *and* **LYLA'S DAD**) *and* **YOUNGER BROTHER, BOBBY***)*

LYLA. Oh no. *(stands facing the wall)*

SADIE. What is it?

LYLA. My parents. I am mortified already!

LYLA'S MOM. *(holding camera)* Hey workin' girl!

LYLA. Hey Mom. I thought we…you said that…you're here!

> (**LYLA'S MOM** *starts to take pictures.*)

LYLA'S MOM. Aww, you didn't think we'd miss our little girl's first day at work did you? That's just silly. Get together!

LYLA. Yes. How silly. *(grimaces as* **MOM** *takes a picture of her and* **LYLA***)*

LYLA'S DAD. *(to* **SADIE***)* How's my little girl brewing? A big summer job! She hasn't burned the place down yet has she? The coffee is looking perky. *(laughs while* **LYLA** *smiles into space blinded by the flashes of the camera.)*

LYLA. Dad, get out of here!

LYLA'S DAD. What, honey?

LYLA. *(changing mood)* Dad, get over here! For a picture!

LYLA'S MOM. What a great idea! *(to* **SADIE***)* Here would you take a picture for us?

SADIE. Sure.

LYLA. This is Sadie, the owner.

LYLA'S DAD. It is Perky in here after all.

LYLA. What?

LYLA'S MOM. Richard.

LYLA'S DAD. What? She seems so nice.

LYLA'S MOM. Fix your shirt.

LYLA'S DAD. I can't see what's always wrong with it.

LYLA'S MOM. I have the perfect frame for this occasion.

LYLA. Is it the one that looks like flames burning in hell?

LYLA'S MOM. What?

LYLA. Is it the one with the flamingos bathing in the shell?

LYLA'S MOM. I'm not sure I know that one…but I'll keep and eye out for it honey. Good idea. Bobby, come over and hug your sister. I see you, what are you looking at over there?

BOBBY. *(facing the door)* The car.

LYLA'S MOM. Get over here. Maybe you can convince your sister to make you a special hot chocolate.

BOBBY. Mom, it's July. I wanted a lemonade! You can't have Hot Chocolate in July!

LYLA'S MOM. Come on over here Bobby, we'll send this out to everyone. Lyla put your chin down. That's right honey. Are you not wearing makeup? Oh, it doesn't matter, you're a working girl now.

LYLA. Thank you, Mom.

LYLA'S DAD. Everyone say "Perky Coffee Beans!"

LYLA AND BOBBY. No, Dad. No. *(shaking their heads)*

LYLA'S MOM. Chin down, honey, you'll thank me later.

LYLA. Not likely.

LYLA'S MOM. What dear?

LYLA. Look lively, Bobby.

*(**BOBBY** scowls at her.)*

SADIE. Okay, 1, 2, 3. Wait, did it take?

LYLA'S MOM. Oh, you have to hold it down for a few seconds.

LYLA'S DAD. She's not a trained photographer Linda. *(laughs)*

LYLA'S MOM. Thank you, Richard. Nice, really nice.

LYLA'S DAD. Ah, Sarah knows I'm just jokin' around.

LYLA. It's Sadie, Dad. Seriously.

LYLA'S DAD. That's what I said honey.

SADIE. Okay. 1, 2…

LYLA'S MOM. Can you make sure that you get the coffee maker in the background. The menu too if you can. It's okay if you cut off our feet a little bit.

SADIE. Sure. 1, 2, 3. Cheese.

LYLA'S MOM. Bobby, did you smile?

BOBBY. Yeah, Mom.

LYLA'S MOM. Good, honey. What a beautiful moment. We are so proud of you, Lyla.

SONG 5 - "HER FIRST DAY"

DAD.

DO YOU REMEMBER WHEN, SHE TOOK HER FIRST BREATH?
I THINK OF IT DAY AND NIGHT.

MOM.

DO YOU REMEMBER WHEN, SHE LAUGHED HER FIRST
    LAUGH,
THAT SMILE THAT SHINES SO BRIGHT!

BOTH.

HER FIRST DAY!
WHO WOULD HAVE THOUGHT IT WOULD COME SO FAST?
HER FIRST DAY!
I WISH THAT IT WOULD LAST AND LAST!

(**LYLA** *groans.*)

MOM.

DO YOU REMEMBER WHEN, SHE HAD HER FIRST BURP?

LYLA. Mom!

MOM.

SHE SPOILED MY BRAND NEW DRESS.

LYLA. Come on!

DAD.

DO YOU REMEMBER WHEN SHE WET HER NEW BED?

LYLA. Dad!

DAD.

BOY THAT WAS QUITE A MESS!!

LYLA. Seriously!

BOTH.

HER FIRST DAY!
WHO WOULD HAVE THOUGHT IT WOULD COME SO FAST?
HER FIRST DAY!
I WISH THAT IT WOULD LAST AND LAST!

MOM.

DO YOU REMEMBER WHEN SHE HAD HER FIRST DATE?
NOW THAT WAS A STAND UP BOY!

LYLA. I can't believe this is still happening.

DAD.

DO YOU REMEMBER WHEN SHE TOTALED THE TRUCK?
AND LEARNED A CAR'S NOT A TOY!

BOTH.

> HER FIRST DAY!
> WHO WOULD HAVE THOUGHT IT WOULD COME SO FAST?
> HER FIRST DAY!
> I WISH THAT IT WOULD LAST AND LAST!

LYLA.

> I LOVE MY PARENTS BUT RIGHT NOW,
> I WISH THAT THEY WEREN'T HERE.
> I LOVE MY FOLKS BUT WHEN THEY SPEAK,
> I COULD JUST DISSAPEAR!

PARENTS.

> HER FIRST DAY!
> WHO WOULD HAVE THOUGHT IT WOULD COME SO FAST!
> HER FIRST DAY!
> I WISH THAT IT WOULD LAST AND LAST!

BOBBY.

> LEMONADE!
> LEMONADE! YOU PROMISED ME SOME LEMONADE!
> LEMONADE, LEMONADE, YOU PROMISED ME SOME
>   LEMONADE!

(Music repeats with **PARENTS** *and* **KIDS** *overlapping.)*

(after round is over:)

ALL.

> BUT
> ALL IN ALL WE LOVE YOU, ON YOUR FIRST DAY!

LYLA. Guys, I really have to get back to work. Right, Sadie?

SADIE. Oh it's okay, I've got it.

*(***LYLA*** glares at her.)*

Actually…come to think of it, I could use some help restacking the…cups.

LYLA'S MOM. Oh, we wouldn't want to interrupt our hard-working daughter.

LYLA'S DAD. That's right. Remember. A coffee sold is a coffee earned.

LYLA. Sure, Dad.

*(***LYLA'S MOM*** takes a picture.)*

LYLA'S MOM. Bye dear. We love you! Richard, grab a couple Splenda.

LYLA. Bye guys.

SADIE. It was great to meet you.

LYLA'S MOM. Bye!

LYLA'S DAD. It's "bean" real!

(**LYLA** *laughs*)

LYLA. Oh, haha Dad. I get it. Clever. Never heard that one before.

(**LYLA'S FAMILY** *exits*)

SADIE. Wow, that's really nice your family came to visit.

(The lights dim down, and customers walk in and out of the store. The "BARISTA SONG" plays and as the lights come up **CUSTOMERS 2** *and* **3** *enter.)*

SONG 6 - "BARISTA SONG REPRISE"

CUSTOMERS.

GOOD AFTERNOON!

(sip) AH!

GOOD AFTERNOON!
THIS NEEDED SIP HELPS ME ESPRESSO MYSELF!
I'VE HAD THREE ALREADY,
MY HAND IS NOT STEADY
UNTIL I HAVE HAD MY FOURTH!
MY BLOOD PRESSURE'S GONE OFF THE CHARTS...
CAFFEINE CAN'T BE GOOD FOR MY HEART!

CUSTOMER 2. But you've seen a chicken. Right?

CUSTOMER 3. Well yeah. *(to* **LYLA AND SADIE***)* Good morning.

LYLA AND SADIE. Good morning/morning.

CUSTOMER 2. But you've never been on a farm.

CUSTOMER 3. I'll have...um... *(ignoring* **CUSTOMER 2***)* I'll have a large decaf caramel mocha skim latte...

CUSTOMER 2. You've never been on a farm, right?

CUSTOMER 3. With honey, not sugar and um, oh ice that, but with half the amount of ice you would usually put. *(to* **CUSTOMER 2***)* Well, no.

CUSTOMER 2. Oh. But you've seen a chicken.

CUSTOMER 3. I mean, I couldn't describe one thoroughly. Umm… And he'll have. What do you want?

CUSTOMER 2. Oh yes, I'll have a large soy chai please. Thanks, ooh and one of those delicious muffins. *(to* **CUSTOMER 3***)* Have you seen a chicken?

CUSTOMER 3. Yeah. I've seen a chicken. Like, at the zoo.

LYLA. Here's your coffee and your muffins.

CUSTOMER 2. At the zoo?

CUSTOMER 3. Yeah, like petting zoos.

CUSTOMER 2. Petting zoos? Why would you pet a chicken?

CUSTOMER 3. Listen, I don't know, okay? I just know that I think I've seen one there. Or something.

CUSTOMER 2. I can't believe you lied about this. And to that old man?

CUSTOMER 3. I panicked okay?

LYLA. Here's your coffee.

CUSTOMER 3. Oh, yeah, thanks. Gosh, I love these muffins.

CUSTOMER 2. You didn't even know him.

CUSTOMER 3. Well, now he thinks he's met someone who really likes poultry. I'm never going to see him again.

CUSTOMER 2. It's your life, man.

LYLA. Bye.

> (**CUSTOMERS** *enter.* **SADIE** *attends to them while* **LYLA** *walks over to* **KEVIN** *who is sitting with his head in his hands.* **CUSTOMERS** *sit down also.)*

LYLA. Hey, Kevin.

KEVIN. Oh, hi.

LYLA. So, you're a musician?

KEVIN. Singer/Songwriter.

LYLA. What kinds of songs do you write?

KEVIN. Just songs about life and love and life and stuff like that.

LYLA. Will you play me one?

KEVIN. Well, I would, but I haven't actually finished one. I need to finish it. If I don't then the woman I love will never know how I feel about her. If I don't tell her now, I'll die. This is my only chance, but I keep putting it off. I mostly just sit here trying to write, but I never get around to it. They say write what you know. I don't know very much. I'm really good at putting things off.

LYLA. Yeah me, too. I have like five books to read this summer, but I haven't even started yet. I know I should, but I just do other things instead.

KEVIN. Me too! I'm the king of procrastinating.

LYLA. Why don't you write a song about that? It's your life!

KEVIN. I guess I could…

LYLA. Just do it. There's barely anyone in here at all.

SONG 7 - "PROCRASTINATION"

KEVIN.

PROCRASTINATION, PROCRASTINATION,
I'M GONNA WRITE A SONG ABOUT PROCRASTINATION.
PROCRASTINATION, PROCRASINATION,
I HAVEN'T WRITTEN THE LYRICS JUST YET.
IT'S SOMETHING LIKE:
LA LA LA LA LA LA LA LA LA LA LA LA LA LA LA LA LA LA LA
    LA
I THINK IT WILL BE, WELL I HOPE IT WILL BE,
SOMETHING GOOD, I'M SURE IT WILL BE.
PROCRASTINATION, PROCRASTINATION,
I'LL WRITE THE LYRICS IN A LITTLE BIT,
THEN I WILL WRITE SOME BRIDGE TO THE SONG,
BUT AFTER I RELACE THE LACES OF THE SHOES I NEVER
    WEAR.
BUT THAT'S BESIDE THE POINT.

I THINK I'LL DO THAT TOMORROW ANYWAY.....
LA LA LA LA LA LA LA LA LA LA LA LA LA LA LA LA LA LA
 LA
I'M CUTTING IT CLOSE, YES I'M CUTTING IT CLOSE.
I'M GONNA WRITE A SONG ABOUT PROCRASTINATION.
I THINK I'LL WRITE THE ENDING A LITTLE LATER
STILL HAVEN'T WRITTEN THE LYRICS JUST YET
SOMETHING LIKE:
(**LYLA** *joins in*)

LA LA LA LA LA LA LA LA LA LA LA LA LA LA LA LA LA LA
 LA

LYLA. So what's the title?

KEVIN. I haven't gotten around to writing it yet.

LYLA. Good one. High Five!

SADIE. Alright, Kevin!

KEVIN. I've got to go find something to write this down! I'll
be back later!

(exits)

(Enter **BRIDE**. *She has been crying. She looks around
with no idea of what she is doing. Her whole world is
confusion. She starts to walk to the counter where* **SADIE**
and **LYLA** *are watching her with a hidden interest. Right
as she gets to the counter she turns around and sits on
a table looking though her purse for a tissue. She finds
an old used one. It is from a roll of toilet paper and she
shakes it out to reveal how much is has been used. It is
all crumpled and soggy. She heaves a sigh and blows her
nose. She sits for a while composing herself and finally
gets up.)*

BRIDE. Hi.

SADIE. Hello. Are you alright?

BRIDE. Yes I'm fine. I'll be fine.

SADIE. What would you like?

BRIDE. I'm getting married tomorrow.

SADIE. *(nonplussed)* Congratulations.

BRIDE. Thank you. *(tries to hold back tears)* I'll have a soy latte. *(Her voice cracks at "soy" but she loses it entirely at latte)* I'm sorry.

*(She reaches for the tissue in her purse, but **SADIE** gives her a fresh napkin instead.)*

Thanks. *(wiping her eyes. She sits down.)*

SADIE. *(following her)* Hey, what's the matter? Are you nervous? Scared? What's wrong?

BRIDE. *(Pauses for a moment, gathering her thoughts. She looks at **SADIE** to see if she will listen)* I just. I'm twenty-four right? And we've been dating for two and a half years *(taking a shaky breath)* and he's a really great, nice, and outgoing guy.

SADIE. That sounds good.

BRIDE. I know! *(starts to cry again)*

SADIE. But what's wrong?

*(**BRIDE** keeps crying. **SADIE** looks around thinking of something to say)*

Being married is a wonderful thing.

BRIDE. *(looking up for encouragement)* Are you married?

SADIE. Well, I was. He passed on a year after we got married. Wow. That was four years ago.

*(**BRIDE** starts crying more.)*

It's okay! It's okay! I just got unlucky that's all.

BRIDE. I'm so sorry. I shouldn't be talking to you about my problems when you have real life drama. Idiot! Idiot! Idiot!

SADIE. Stop! Stop! Your life is important. This conversation took a serious turn, didn't it? I'm sure you and your fiancé will be married for a long time.

BRIDE. *(starts crying again)* Yeah. Probably.

SADIE. What's wrong with that?

*(**SADIE** gets up to get **BRIDE**'s drink.)*

BRIDE. I don't know. But for some reason, thinking about it makes me cry. A lot.

SADIE. Hold on. Take a deep breath.

(**SADIE** *hands* **BRIDE** *her drink.* **BRIDE** *breathes a shaky breath.*)

No deeper. With me.

(*They breathe together.*)

BRIDE. We don't have any money.

SADIE. So? You'll get some.

BRIDE. Oh. But I'll never be with another man…you know…again.

SADIE. Do you want to?

BRIDE. (*starting to cry again*) Maybe? I don't know, I just said that because that's what everyone says.

SADIE. Hmmm…

BRIDE. But, how do I know he's the right one? What happens if he's not?

SADIE. I can't tell you.

(*Underscore for WHO DO YOU LOVE begins.*)

But I can ask you this:

SONG 8 -"WHO DO YOU LOVE?"

WHO DO YOU LOVE? WHO'S THE ONE WHO YOU DREAM OF?
TELL ME WHO? WHO?
WHO IS AROUND WHEN YOU NEED THAT SOMEONE,
TO LOVE YOU?
WHO WOULD YOU RUN TO IF HE ASKED YOU TO?
WHO KNOW'S YOU'D BE THERE?
AND WHO WOULD CHOOSE YOU IF HIS CHOICE WAS BUT
  ONE?
WHO? TELL ME WHO?
AND WHO IS THE ONE WHO YOU KNOW YOU CAN CLING
  TO,
WHEN YOU MUST BE STRONG ALL ALONE?
AND WHO IS THE ONE TO MAKE YOUR HEART ALWAYS SEEM
  NEW?
WHO KNOWS YOUR SECRETS BETTER THAN YOU?
WHO WOULD COME RUNNING IF YOU ASKED HIM TO?

TO CATCH YOU WHEN YOU FALL?
AND WHO WOULD YOU CHOOSE IF YOUR CHOICE WAS BUT
    ONE?
WHO? TELL ME WHO?
AND WHO IS THE ONE WHO YOUR HEART ONLY THINKS OF?
TELL ME WHO?
TELL ME WHO?
YOU KNOW WHO.

BRIDE. You know what? You're right! I'm gonna do it! I'm going to marry Jon!

SADIE. That's the attitude!

BRIDE. I'll call right now. *(She dials.)* Michael, it's me. The engagement's off. *(She pauses.)* So…I guess give me a call when you get this. Talk to you later. Bye.

SADIE. What?

BRIDE. I do love Jon. He's always been there. He's the one I love!

SADIE. Who is Jon? He's not your fiancé?

BRIDE. Oh no! Jon is Michael's brother. *(starting to pack up to go)*

SADIE. Wow. I had no idea. I thought you were just having the pre-wedding jitters.

BRIDE. I don't know why I haven't done this sooner! I love Jon! Not Michael! Thank you for helping me. I know what I need to do. *(starts calling Jon)* Oh, wait.

(She remembers to pay for drink. She gets out her wallet while holding her phone with her shoulder)

SADIE. It's on me.

BRIDE. *(mouthing)* Thank you. *(to phone)* Oh, Jon? It's me. What are you doing? Can I come over? I have something to say. Okay great.

(exits smiling and waving happily)

*(**SADIE** and **LYLA** all stare at each other for a moment in disbelief.)*

LYLA. Hey, Sadie, are you alright?

SADIE. I'm fine. I haven't talked about him in a while. You only have so much time with people. You're all going off to college soon, and who knows who will still be your friend in a couple of years. The brevity of life is something to embrace. Allow it to move you to take risks. I opened this coffee shop because I wanted to. It was a risk, but now I'm happy. I love it. Plus I'm single now, right? Haha. Terrible joke.

LYLA. That was an unfortunate thing to say.

SADIE. You know what?

LYLA. What?

SADIE. All this talk about love and stuff reminds me of something.

LYLA. What?

(SADIE looks at her.)

Me and Justin? No. It won't happen.

SADIE. Not if you don't make it happen. You don't have forever.

(enter KAT, LYLA's best friend)

KAT. There she is!!! Oh my gosh, you look sooo cute in that little apron! Hi!!!

LYLA. Hi Kat!! Welcome to the Perky Coffee Bean!

(She runs out from behind the counter and they squeal and hug.)

This is Sadie, the owner. Sadie, this is my best friend Kat!

SADIE. Cute purse, Kat!

KAT. Cute coffee shop, Sadie!

SADIE. Would you like a drink?

KAT. Can you make caramel lattes?

SADIE. Anything your heart desires. It's a welcome gift from me. Put your purse down.

KAT. Thank you. This is the nicest place ever.

LYLA. Kat! I have to tell you. You're not going to believe this.

KAT. Dan and Jenny were caught in the teacher's lounge during summer school?

LYLA. Eeew. Dan Carter? No. That's not at all what I was going to say. Hold on. Jenny! Come on! Dan? No, no, no! I have to tell you something absolutely amazing about me!

KAT. Spill.

LYLA. Justin Baker is giving me a ride home tonight!

KAT. Oh my gosh! You did it! You asked him out!

LYLA. I didn't ask him out.

KAT. I thought that was the reason you decided to work here.

LYLA. What? No, it's not! Kat!

KAT. He's giving you a ride home! He's giving you a ride home!

(They squeal and jump up and down.)

SADIE. So you know Justin, too? I didn't know he was such a hot item.

KAT. He is to Lyla. She has been desperately trying to get him to notice her for years now.

SONG 9 - "LYLA'S GOT THE MOVES"

YOU WOULD THINK BECAUSE SHE'S OFTEN FAIRLY KLUTZY
SHE WOULD NOT BE SUCH A CHARMER WITH THE BOYS.
DON'T LET HER AWKWARD NATURE MISINFORM YOU.
I'LL TELL YOU RIGHT NOW THAT
LYLA'S GOT THE MOVES
IN MIDDLE SCHOOL AT THE ALL SCHOOL FORMAL,
YOU COULD SEE HER START TO GET INTO THE GROOVE.
HER STILLETTO JABBED HIS TOE, WHICH WAS A BUMMER.
I THINK YOU SEE THAT LYLA'S GOT THE MOVES.
SHE WAS RUNNING DOWN THE HALLWAY WITH HER PAPERS,
WHEN SHE FELL AND THEY FLEW ALL OVER THE PLACE,
WHEN JUSTIN CAME TO HELP HER SHE GOT NERVOUS.
SHE STOOD UP TOO FAST AND WHAPPED HIM IN THE FACE.

KAT. *(cont.)*
   JUSTIN'S HANDSOME, LYLA'S A CATCH.
   EVERYONE CAN SEE IT!
   THEY MAKE AN ADORABLE MATCH.
   YOU SHOULD WATCH HIM WHEN SHE'S TELLING HIM A
      STORY,
   WHEN SHE TRIPS ON WORDS OR LAUGHS HIS MOOD
      IMPROVES,
   ALTHOUGH HE ACTS TOO COOL TO EVEN NOTICE,
   I CAN SEE HE'S DIGGING LYLA'S MOVES.
   OH YES, BELIEVE ME YOU, OUR LYLA'S GOT THE MOVES.

SADIE. I think I saw some of those more unfortunate moves earlier today.

KAT. Excellent. So did she stutter when he came in? I love that. "Huh-huh-huh-hi, Justin."

SADIE. Hilarious. Not really. She went cold turkey.

KAT. I love that one too! The one sided conversation with her.

SADIE. Yes! Precisely!

KAT. I've got to run. Keep me updated if anything happens. Here's my number. Text me if she throws up on him or something.

SADIE. Will do.

LYLA. Now there's a conspiracy against me. Lovely.

KAT. Tootle Lyliees. Great to meet you, Sadie. I'll be coming in here all the time.

SADIE. Love it!

KAT. Bye, Lyla!!

   *(**KAT** exits.)*

SADIE. You have to tell him.

LYLA. I can't!

SADIE. He's driving you home right?

LYLA. Yes.

SADIE. So, tell him tonight!

LYLA. *(in a fit of giggles)* No!!!!

SADIE. If you don't, I will.

LYLA. No you wouldn't.

SADIE. Bet you a hundred dollars. *(sticking out hand)*

LYLA. I'm not going to bet you.

SADIE. You know you want to tell him.

LYLA. What do I say?

SADIE. How about, I like you? Something to that effect?

> *(**LYLA** sighs and sits in her chair.)*

> Here, practice on me.

LYLA. Okay.

> *(**SADIE** gets up and stands by the door.)*

SADIE. *(as **JUSTIN**)* I've come to pick you up, Lyla.

LYLA. Are you serious?

SADIE. Please play along. Do you think I'm enjoying this?

LYLA. Actually, yes.

SADIE. Pretend, Lyla!

LYLA. Hi, Justin. *(rolling her eyes)*

SADIE. Ready to go home?

LYLA. Yes. Okay, let's go.

SADIE. *(making a buzzer sound)* Wrong!

LYLA. I was going to tell him in the car.

SADIE. You have to tell him here.

LYLA. What? Why?

SADIE. Because I'm going to hide behind the counter to make sure you do it.

LYLA. What? Why?

SADIE. Because you won't do it otherwise.

LYLA. Really? You'd do that for me?

SADIE. Yeah. For moral support. And I want to hear.

LYLA. Oh man…okay. Let's start over.

SADIE. *(back at the door)* Hi, Lyla. Ready to go home?

LYLA. Hold on, Justin…

SADIE. Yes?

SONG 10 - "ON MY MIND"

LYLA.

> YOU'RE TOO OFTEN ON MY MIND.
> YOU'RE IN TOO MANY DREAMS.
> AND WHEN I THINK OF YOU,
> IT'S ALL I CAN DO.
> I DON'T WANT YOU TO BE NEAR.
> I DON'T WANT YOU AT ALL.
> BUT I CAN'T EXPLAIN THIS NEED,
> TO HEAR YOU LAUGHING.
> PLEASE DON'T LOOK AT ME SO MUCH.
> PLEASE DON'T LOOK AT ME THAT WAY.
> PLEASE DON'T LOOK AT ME AT ALL.
> BUT DON'T TURN AWAY.
> WHEN YOU WALK INTO A ROOM.
> YOU ARE ALL THAT I SEE,
> AND I WONDER IF YOU SENSE
> THAT I AM THINKING
> ABOUT YOU IN THE MORNING
> AND OF YOU WHEN STARS APPEAR
> IT IS YOU WHO I ADORE,
> BUT HOW COULD YOU KNOW?

> *(At key change, she boldly steps to* **SADIE***)*

> YOU'RE TOO OFTEN ON MY MIND.
> YOU'RE IN ALL OF MY DREAMS.
> AND ALL I WANT TO DO
> IS BE WITH YOU.

SADIE. Lyla, that was really lovely.

LYLA. Thanks.

SADIE. If you do it like that. He will totally kiss you.

LYLA. Okay! I'll do it!

SADIE. Now there are a couple of scenarios that can happen. One. He walks in and you say, "Justin, I like you, I've liked you since forever, and now I'm going to kiss you." Then you kiss him. "Will you go out with me?" and he says, "I love you too and I want to date you." Two. He walks in the door. You kiss him. Love. Maybe a little lust too. Getting down and dirty on the coffee shop floor.

LYLA. Eewww Sadie!

SADIE. No? Okay, Three. He could come in and then you guys would get caught up in a conversation and you would make him a drink and he would give you a muffin that he made especially for you and he would say: "I have to tell you, but oh! I can't do it!" and you would say, "What is it?" pretending like you didn't know what he was going to say (although you already knew) and he'd say, "Well," and you'd say, "Yes," and move in closer to him and he would say, "Will you be my girlfriend?" and you'd say, "Yes!" and then you'd make out, while I quietly left because I wouldn't want to be in the same room as that, as much as I love you and all, and oh my God someone's coming in!!!

*(**LYLA** ducks behind the counter or table. **KEVIN** walks in. **SADIE** drops to the floor as is she has heard a gun shot. Silence.)*

KEVIN. Um, hello? Is anyone here?

*(**LYLA** slowly pokes her head out from behind the counter and stands up slowly smiling at **KEVIN**.)*

LYLA. *(pretends to pick up something from the counter)* There it is.

KEVIN. There's what?

LYLA. *(acting like she didn't know he was there)* Oh, hey Kevin. What's up?

KEVIN. What are you doing? Is Sadie here? I thought you were just talking to someone.

LYLA. Yes….I was. *(kicking **SADIE**)* Stand up!

SADIE. Yes. *(stands up)* I'm here. Hey Kevin.

KEVIN. Hello Sadie. *(stares)*

SADIE. How are you? *(blushing)*

KEVIN. Good. *(still staring but catches himself and looks away)* I just forgot my pick, it's the one I got at the Allman Brother's concert and I really need it.

SADIE. I was at that concert too!

KEVIN. Really?

(**LYLA** *sees it on the ground and hands it to* **SADIE,** **SADIE** *takes it.*)

SADIE. Is this it?

KEVIN. Thanks. (**SADIE** *smiles.*) Okay bye.

(*Exits.* **LYLA** *is aware something is happening.*)

LYLA. What were you saying, Sadie?

SADIE. Oh, um, Justin. (*obviously distracted*)

(**KEVIN** *bursts back in and walks up to* **SADIE,** *grabs her hand then immediately lets it go.*)

KEVIN. Sadie, I like you. I've liked you since forever and now I'm going to kiss you.

(*They kiss.*)

Will you be my girlfriend?

LYLA. (*throws her hands up in the air*) What?!

SADIE. Oh Kevin, I never knew!

KEVIN. That song I've been trying to write…I wanted to write it for you, but I never could.

SADIE. That song about procrastination?

KEVIN. Well, in a way, yes.

(**JUSTIN** *enters and waves at* **LYLA,** *but waits at the door so as not to disturb* **SADIE** *and* **KEVIN.**)

(**LYLA** *feels extremely uncomfortable. She could just melt away. It's like when you're out on a date with a boy you hardly know and you happen to have chosen the most romantic and cheesy and depressing chick flick out in theatres and you have to sit right next to him the whole time, thinking that you can never find a way to tell him that you like him especially after seeing such a horribly romantic movie, and you want to cry but you can't because he's right next to you. It's like that.*)

SONG 11 - "PROCRASTINATION REFRAIN"

SADIE & KEVIN. *(slowly)*

> LA, LA, LA, LA, LA, LA, LA, LA, LA, LA, LA, LA, LA, LA, LA, LA, LA, LA, LA,
> LA, LA, LA, LA, LA, LA, LA, LA.

KEVIN. I didn't know how to say it, but I had to. I just had to.

SADIE. Oh Kevin.

> *(Kiss again. **JUSTIN** looks at **LYLA** who looks back and then hastily looks away. **JUSTIN** fidgets and looks around the room.)*

LYLA. Uh, Sadie? *(glances at **JUSTIN**)* I guess I'll see you tomorrow. I'm closing tonight.

SADIE. *(Turning to look at **JUSTIN** as well)* Oh yeah. Ooh!!! Are you okay to do this?

LYLA. Yeah. I think.

SADIE. I'll just clean up tomorrow if you miss stuff. *(To **KEVIN**)* Want to go watch a foreign film?

KEVIN. Oh, Yes!

> *(They exit.)*

> *(**LYLA** and **JUSTIN** are left alone in the room.)*

JUSTIN. So Sadie and Kevin are together now?

LYLA. Yep.

JUSTIN. Hey, I really want to tell you something….

LYLA. Yes?

> *(enter **LYLA'S MOM**)*

LYLA'S MOM. Hi Lyla! We came to pick you up! Did you have a good time? Your father's out in the car, he didn't want to find a parking space so he's just sitting at the curb holding up traffic. So it was a good day?

LYLA. Yeah. A great day. But mom, I got a ride.

LYLA'S MOM. Really? Did you text your father?

LYLA. Yeah! Five times.

LYLA'S MOM. Well, I'm sure it's easier if we gave you one… is that Justin Baker?

JUSTIN. Hi, Linda. How are you?

LYLA'S MOM. Justin! You are so handsome! Come get a hug! What great news. My little bride and her groom reunited!

JUSTIN. Yeah! Remember that? We got married!

LYLA. Why is this happening?

(She turns away to hide her embarrassment.)

LYLA'S MOM. Oh, this is just perfect. Why don't you get together? Justin, do you work here as well?

LYLA. He's the Muffin Man.

LYLA'S MOM. How lovely.

JUSTIN. Yeah. *(laughs)* I am the muffin man, I guess.

LYLA'S MOM. Smile!

(She takes the picture, they smile. **JUSTIN** *puts his arm around* **LYLA.** *They linger for a moment after the picture is taken.)*

We can give you a ride home, Justin. Do you need one? I would love to see your mother.

JUSTIN. Oh thank you, but I have a car.

LYLA'S MOM. Well, then we can take Lyla. It's no problem. It was really sweet of you to offer.

LYLA. Mom. I have a ride. Justin already offered.

LYLA'S MOM. Well, it looks like you are very intent on having him drive you home. Don't keep her out too late, Justin.

JUSTIN. Don't worry, Linda. I'll have her home before midnight.

LYLA'S MOM. Oh haha. How sweet. What a charming young man. So now, where are you going to college?

JUSTIN. Dartmouth.

LYLA'S MOM. Hold on one second. *(She gets her cell phone which is vibrating in her pocket and takes a long look at who is calling.)* Oh it's Bobby. I better get this. One moment.

Bobby. Where are you? Are you not with your father in the car? No, you may not. Bobby. Nope. Bobby. Bobby? Yes, she's right there. Bobby, now calm down. Bobby? Bobby?...I guess we lost service. So, Darmouth? Congratulations! And he's smart, Lyla. *(winks)*

LYLA. Mom. Please. Don't you have to go… anywhere?

LYLA'S MOM. Oh Lyla. So, tell me about your end of senior year. Was it so much fun? Give me all the details.

(enter **BOBBY***)*

BOBBY. Mom! Dad's getting another ticket.

LYLA'S MOM. Richard? What is he doing? Justin? Can you take Lyla home?

JUSTIN. I'd love to.

LYLA. Love to…

LYLA'S MOM. Excellent. Thank you so much. We really appreciate it. Bobby? Come here.

BOBBY. Mom!

(They exit.)

LYLA. *(moving away from* **JUSTIN***)* I'll just finish up okay, Justin?

JUSTIN. Can I help?

LYLA. I'm almost done. Do you want something to drink?

JUSTIN. No thanks. *(sits down)*

LYLA. Okay. *(waits a moment to gain courage then quietly sings:)* WHY DO WE PONDER AND WORRY…

(trails off)

JUSTIN. What did you say?

LYLA. Nothing. *(embarrassed)*

JUSTIN. You're just singing to yourself?

LYLA. Yep. *(hums to herself)*

JUSTIN. Cool.

LYLA. Well…no.

(Enter **GARY** *again,* **JUSTIN** *steps to the side.)*

GARY. Good Evening, Lyla. Are you closed yet?

LYLA. Just about.

GARY. I'll have a coffee. You haven't sold out of those muffins yet, have you?

LYLA. Looks like we have one left.

GARY. Lucky me!

LYLA. Lucky you.

GARY. I don't have to pay for this, right? Yum. Delicious. So, how's your boy?

LYLA. *(freezes, looking over to* **JUSTIN***)* My what?

GARY. That boy you have a crush on. Remember we talked earlier. Your little bridegroom.

LYLA. *(switches on the coffee grinder while he is speaking, yells over the noise)* I don't know what you are talking about.

GARY. What?

LYLA. I can't hear you.

GARY. What?

> *(***LYLA*** moves out of sight from* **JUSTIN***, motions: Stop! He's right over there!!!!!)*

GARY. *(looks over at* **JUSTIN***)* Oh..........

JUSTIN. *(leans around to look at what* **LYLA** *is doing)* ....

LYLA. *(Changes her movements to seem like she isn't pointing at him. The coffee grinder is still on.)* I don't know what you're saying.

GARY. *(catches on)* I was saying, how is your soy...milk? Do you have soy?

LYLA. Oh soy!

GARY. Soy.

LYLA. Yes, we do have soy milk. *(turns off coffee grinder)*

GARY. Oh boy!

> *(He pays her and exits)*

LYLA. Bye. *(She continues to clean.)*

JUSTIN. So is your family coming to our Labor Day party again?

LYLA. I think so. That's about two months from now though, so I don't really know.

JUSTIN. It is.

LYLA. *(Coming out from behind the counter.)* Justin?

JUSTIN. Yeah?

SONG 12 - "I'M GOING TO TELL YOU"

LYLA.

I REALIZED THIS MORNING,
WHEN YOU WALKED THROUGH THE DOOR
I KNOW WHAT MY LIFE IS FOR.
I WISH THAT I COULD TELL YOU
WHAT I'M FEELING FOR YOU
YOU MEAN THE WORLD TO ME.

*(**LYLA** realizes what she just said and starts to freak out. She starts pacing around the store and avoiding **JUSTIN***'s eye contact. She fidgets and is extremely nervous. She starts to sweat.)*

I HAVE NEVER SAID WHAT I AM TRYING TO SAY TO
YOU ARE AN OLD FRIEND SO PLEASE DON'T TAKE THIS THE
WRONG

(aside) WAY TOO MANY WORDS HE'S GONNA WALK
RIGHT OUT THE

*(to **JUSTIN**)* (DOOR)-DURING WORK MY FRIEND TOLD
ME THAT YOU MIGHT LIKE ME

TOO (TO) GIVE YOU A CUP OF COFFEE BUT HEY! YOU LIKE
TEA,
I'M JUST BEING FUNNY HAHA HA HA OH GOD.

(aside) I'VE HEARD THE WORD IDIOTIC BEFORE, BUT I
JUST NOW KNOW WHAT IT MEANS.

*(to **JUSTIN**)* I AM GOING TO DO IT TELL YOU HOW I
FEEL RIGHT

NOW I'M REALLY SWEATING, ARE YOU HOT, I'M REALLY HOT,
I MEAN I NEED TO BREATHE I'M REALLY REALLY REALLY
REALLY REALLY REALLY REALLY, STOP!

(music stops)

LYLA.

> I'M GOING TO TELL YOU.
> I REALLY LIKE YOU.
> I DO!

LYLA. *(at downbeat)* So, do you like me too?

JUSTIN. I don't know what to say.

LYLA. I knew it. I knew it!! Ugh! I shouldn't have said anything!

JUSTIN. No! Not at all. I just. It's just that.

(underscore for "On My Mind Reprise")

Since I saw you this morning....

SONG 13 - "ON MY MIND REPRISE"

YOU'RE TOO OFTEN ON MY MIND.
YOU'RE IN TOO MANY DREAMS.
AND WHEN I THINK OF YOU
IT'S ALL I CAN DO.
OH STOP TAKING UP MY THOUGHTS,
OH STOP CLOUDING MY SKIES.
I JUST WANT TO LIVE AND NOT BE BOTHERED.
OH IT'S YOU IN THE MORNING.
OH IT'S YOU BENEATH THE MOON.
OH IT'S YOU IN THE END.
PLEASE DON'T GO AWAY.

LYLA.

> YOU'RE TOO OFTEN ON MY MIND.

JUSTIN.

> YOU'RE IN ALL OF MY DREAMS.

BOTH.

> AND ALL I WANT TO DO, IS BE WITH YOU.

JUSTIN. I am so sorry it has taken such a long time for me to do this.

*(He starts to lean in, **LYLA** stops him.)*

LYLA. Wait. A long time? How long have you felt this way?

JUSTIN. I can't tell you.

LYLA. Why?

JUSTIN. Because, well, I have always known you were the one since we first exchanged baby rings…It's really weird our parents did that.

LYLA. Yeah, it is.

JUSTIN. I mean you're a year younger, so it was kind of hard to keep in touch.

LYLA. I know exactly what you mean.

JUSTIN. But there's been so many times that I've been such a doofus in front of you. I had no idea you would still like me.

LYLA. You're never a doofus. You're so cool!

JUSTIN. Not really… You mean you didn't hear that high pitched yelp when I slammed my finger in the door while I was watching you run into school, you know that day when we had the half day?

LYLA. I don't remember that.

JUSTIN. Really? That's such a relief. Gary still makes fun of me for that. Or that time my fly was down the whole time we were talking during the Bastille Day party?

LYLA. I didn't notice that.

JUSTIN. Wow. You are so cute and perfect and I should have done it earlier, but… *(pause)* what are you doing Saturday night?

LYLA. Nothing.

JUSTIN. Can I take you out?

LYLA. No.

JUSTIN. *(totally thrown off guard)* What? Really?

LYLA. Of course you can.

(*She smiles, blushing, and kisses him on the cheek.*)

JUSTIN. Are you hungry?

LYLA. Yeah, a little.

JUSTIN.
> WELL I'LL MAKE YOU BLUEBERRY MUFFINS, 'CUZ I'M THE MUFFIN MAN,

(**LYLA** *laughs.*)

JUSTIN.

AND YOU CAN TELL EVERYONE HERE THE'YRE MADE JUST
　　FOR YOU!
BUT I HAD TO TELL YOU THE WAY THAT I LOVED YOU
I DON'T EVEN KNEAD THE DOUGH!
My dad does that part anyway, And it's more of a batter
than a it is a dough with muffins…And I don't care
about money. I don't know how you interpreted that
sentence…

LYLA. It's okay.

JUSTIN.

SO, I'LL BE YOUR MUFFIN MAN, YOUR ONE AND ONLY
　　MUFFIN MAN

LYLA.

YOU'RE MY MUFFIN MAN, OH MUFFIN MAN,

BOTH.

I LOVE YOU SO.

(*Turns off the light and locks door.* **JUSTIN** *dips* **LYLA**
and they slip and land on the ground.)

(*end of play*)

PROPERTY PLOT

Stack of hot to-go cups with lids
Stack of cold to-go cups with lids and straws
Tip jar
Blender and ice (to make loud noise)
Espresso maker
2 coffee urns
Pitchers and/or cartons for milk
Condiment Tray
Straws
Yellow sugar substitute packets
Pink sugar substitute packets
White sugar packets
2 aprons
Cleaning rags
Colored chalk
Camera (Lyla's Mom)
Brown Bag lunch (Lyla)
Guitar pick (Kevin)

SET PLOT

Large chalk board with prices of drinks and "The Perky Coffee Bean"
    written on the top
Counter
2-3 small tables
5-6 chairs